uncles and antlers

by **lisa wheeler**

illustrated by **brian floca**

A Richard Jackson Book
Atheneum Books for Young Readers
New York London Toronto Sydney

Seven uncles, every year,
seven uncles, travel here—
shaggy coats, scarves of red,
two tall antlers on each head.

Uncle Uno—first in line—
just flew up from Caroline,
wears lift tickets on each tine . . .
and he's my fastest uncle!

He has **one** hat.

He has **one** vest.

He wears **one** stopwatch on his chest.

He lost **one** pole. He lost **one** ski.

He says his favorite niece is ME!

THANK YOU, THANK YOU VERY MUCH,

Uncle Duce from Cameroon,

bellows out an Elvis tune.

When he sings, the girls all swoon. . . .

And he's my loudest uncle.

He has **two** wigs. He has **two** boots.

He has **two** shiny white jumpsuits.

He has **two** roadies—Gnat and Flea.

He says his favorite niece is ME!

Uncle Trey is short and wide.

Antler tines? Three on each side!

Wears a wetsuit on his hide . . .

and he's my sweetest uncle.

He has **three** masks that hide **three** chins.

He owns **three** sets of swimming fins.

We snorkel every day at **three**.

His favorite niece is—glub-glub—ME!

Uncles **one** and **two** and **three**
electrify the scenery.

Uncle Four-eyes is such fun—
brings me gifts from Galveston.
Says his antlers weigh a ton . . .
and he's my strongest uncle!

YEE-HA!

He has **four** lassos and **four** spurs.
Four-gallon hats—what he prefers!
His rope tricks are a sight to see.

He says his favorite niece is ME.

Uncle Quint is long and tall—
a star of trick-shot basketball.
He dribbled down from Montreal. . . .
And he's my coolest uncle!

WHOOSH! NOTHIN' BUT NET!

He has **five** earrings, **five** tattoos,
and **five** new pairs of brand-name shoes.
He does commercials on TV!

**He
says
his
favorite
niece
is
ME.**

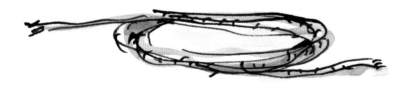

Uncle **four** and uncle **five**
wrap the gifts as snow arrives.

Here comes crazy Uncle Sy.
He's a fearless sort of guy.
Gives most any stunt a try . . .
and he's my bravest uncle!

He has **six** bumps. He has **six** scars.

He has **six** crashed-up racing cars.

He has **six** stitches on his knee.

OUCH!

He says his
favorite niece
is ME.

Last of all comes Uncle Sven,

a literary gentleman,

writes poetry with feathered pen . . .

and he's my smartest uncle!

Seven books and **seven** plays,

seven poems for **seven** days.

When he recites, the uncles cry.

His favorite niece? Well, it is I!

Yay for **seven**!
Yay for **six**!

They're all here now.
It's quite a mix.
Each uncle's cool!
Each uncle's great!

And I'm Octavia—number **eight**.

Eight fine reindeer, every year—
Eight fine reindeer gather here.

We do it once a year because . . .

we pull the sleigh for Santa Claus!

We change our clothes.

We hitch the sleigh.

We're ready now. . . .

We're on our way!